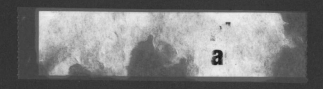

First published in Great Britain in 2007
by Zero To Ten Limited
2A Portman Mansions, Chiltern Street,
London W1U 6NR

This edition © 2007 Zero To Ten Limited
© Gallimard Jeunesse 2006

First published in France in 2006 as
Le Noël de Rita et Machin

British Library Cataloguing in Publication Data:
Arrou-Vignod, Jean-Philippe, 1958-
Christmas with Rita and Whatsit
1. Rita (Fictitious character : Arrou-Vignod) - Juvenile
fiction 2. Whatsit (Fictitious character) - Juvenile
fiction 3. Christmas stories 4. Children's stories
I. Title
843.9'14[J]

ISBN: 9781840895179

Printed in China

JEAN-PHILIPPE ARROU-VIGNOD ✱ OLIVIER TALLEC

ZERO TO TEN

It's the night before Christmas.
Still lots to do to get ready for the day!

Rita and Whatsit write their letters
to Father Christmas.

Whatsit doesn't have many ideas.
He only wants –

a bone to gnaw,

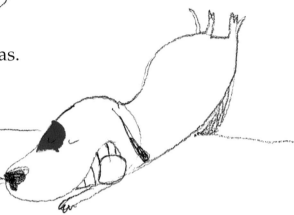

a policeman's outfit,

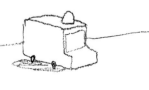

a big pack of biscuits, gym kit, Professor Hound's book
'How to train your mistress in 12 easy lessons'
… and a hundred other things…

'Hey, Whatsit!' scolded Rita. 'That's not how you decorate the tree. You need glass baubles, and streamers and tinsel and lights … stop that and help me or you'll be for it!'

Oh look, what's this in the corner? Hung with thin sausages, and fat sausages, and biscuits, and ham…

It's Whatsit's secret tree.

Quick! Cooking to do. Rita makes
her surprise pudding – chocolate
log with jam sauce.

And don't forget to leave a snack
on the front step for Father
Christmas and his reindeer.

'I'm going to teach you to sing a few carols,'
says Rita. 'We can have a big Christmas Eve
concert.'

But Whatsit sings like a saucepan.
A bit of rock and roll is so much better!

All is now ready. Before going to bed, Rita puts out the stockings. As Whatsit hasn't been a very good dog lately, one old slipper should be enough for him.

But Whatsit has other ideas.

'Hey! Who's pinched Father
Chrismas's snack?'

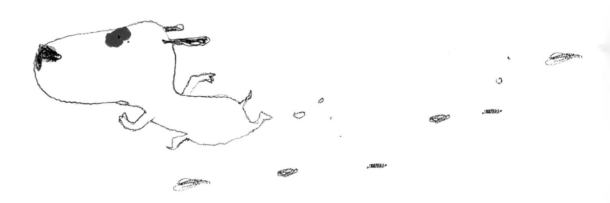

'And the carrots for
the reindeer?'

'Whatsit! Belly on four legs! Just
you wait till I catch you.'

'Off you go, bedtime!' say Mum and Dad.
'And no peeping under the tree until tomorrow morning.'

But a night is such a long time to wait
when it's Christmas Eve.

It's midnight. Everyone is asleep.

Suddenly, there's a noise downstairs, then another.
Someone is in the house…
Super Whatsit, amazing guard dog, to the rescue!

Mind your ankles.
Super Whatsit will attack!

Whatsit, be quiet! I wonder if it's …

Rita and Whatsit tiptoe downstairs.

All is quiet. The visitor has left.

'Disaster!' cries Rita. 'You've frightened
Father Christmas away!'

But, when they open the sitting room door, there,
under the tree, is a huge pile of presents.

Is anything missing?

Just one thing – a big hug from a friend.
Happy Christmas, Rita and Whatsit!